KU-443-541

Rabbit Rescue

A good-sized bunny hutch was sitting in the grass next to the trailer. Miss Piggy was sitting in a cosy pile of hay. The rabbit's eyes were half closed and her fur was messy.

"What do you think?" Red asked.

Stella thought Miss Piggy looked pretty sick but she didn't want to tell Red that. "I think my aunt should look at her," Stella said.

Books available in the **Animal Emergency** series

1. Abandoned Puppy
2. Otter Alert
3. Bad Luck Lion
4. Runaway Wolf
5. Rabbit Rescue

Coming Soon

6. Kitten Crisis   *September 2000*

All of the **Animal Emergency** books
can be ordered at your local bookshop
or are available by post from
Book Service by Post (tel: 01624 675137)

Animal Emergency

Rabbit Rescue

Emily Costello

Illustrated by Diz Wallis

MACMILLAN CHILDREN'S BOOKS

For Julia Jones and Miss Mattie

First published 2000 by Avon Books, USA
a division of HarperCollinsPublishers

This edition published 2000 by Macmillan Children's Books
a division of Macmillan Publishers Limited
25 Eccleston Place, London SW1W 9NF
Basingstoke and Oxford
www.macmillan.co.uk

Associated companies throughout the world

ISBN 0 330 39358 8

Text copyright © Emily Costello 2000
Illustrations copyright © Diz Wallis 2000

The right of Emily Costello to be identified as the
author of this work has been asserted by her in accordance
with the Copyright, Designs and Patents Act 1988.

All rights reserved. No part of this publication may be
reproduced, stored in or introduced into a retrieval system, or
transmitted, in any form, or by any means (electronic, mechanical,
photocopying, recording or otherwise) without the prior written
permission of the publisher. Any person who does any unauthorized
act in relation to this publication may be liable to criminal
prosecution and civil claims for damages.

1 3 5 7 9 8 6 4 2

A CIP catalogue record for this book is available from
the British Library.

Typeset by SX Composing DTP, Rayleigh, Essex
Printed and bound in Great Britain by Mackays of Chatham plc, Kent

This book is sold subject to the condition that it shall not,
by way of trade or otherwise, be lent, re-sold, hired out,
or otherwise circulated without the publisher's prior consent
in any form of binding or cover other than that in which
it is published and without a similar condition including this
condition being imposed on the subsequent purchaser.

The author wishes to thank several generous people who helped make this book stronger. Kenneth Franz of the Boise Smokejumpers shared his vivid tales of watching forest fires develop; Susan Mitchell of Angell Memorial Hospital in Boston told me about treating windpipe injuries in dogs; and Charlene Harris of the Women's Professional Rodeo Association explained a thing or two about barrel racing.

If your pet is unwell, please don't try to treat it yourself. Only a qualified vet can give your pet the care and attention it needs when it's ill. Make sure you keep your vet's telephone number by the phone in case of an emergency, and always ask an adult for help if you find a sick or injured animal. Never approach wild animals – being too close to humans may scare them, and they sometimes bite or carry diseases.

Remember – your pet is your friend. Make sure you look after it properly!

❀ 1 ❀

Stella Sullivan was watching her mother carefully. She wanted to be ready in case Norma needed help. You have to be alert when you're around wild animals.

Norma had hold of a huge chunk of deer meat. She was jerking the meat backwards through a gate and into a big pen. Norma's co-worker Mack was hauling a big piece too.

A motorist had hit the deer out on Route 2A sometime the night before. A park ranger had spotted the carcass early that morning. Norma and Mack had carried the fresh meat to the pen in large, heavy backpacks.

Stella hated to think about deer getting hit by cars. She loved deer. In fact, she loved animals of all sorts. Furry ones. Fuzzy ones. Fierce ones. Gentle ones. Animals that ate plants and animals that ate meat.

She was sad the deer had died. But wolves liked fresh meat.

The pen held nine wolves, eight four-week-old pups and their mother, who was called Juliet. The wolves had run to the back of the pen as soon as Stella, Norma and Mack had come out of the woods. They were doing all they could to stay far, far away from the people.

Everything about the wolves showed their wariness: their posture, the expression in their eyes. The message was loud and clear. People are bad news.

Norma and Mack dropped the deer meat and hurried out of the pen. The wolves didn't pounce on their food. They didn't come even one step closer. Stella knew they wouldn't – not as long as people were hanging around.

Later, after they left, Juliet would stuff herself. She would digest the meat into a high-protein pulp. Then, whenever one of the pups nudged her mouth, she would regurgitate some of the meat for it.

Stella couldn't imagine a more disgusting diet. But the pups were thriving on the meat pulp and their mother's milk. When Stella had first seen the pups three weeks earlier, they were tiny. Helpless. But they'd grown fast. Now they were bigger than Stella's five-month-old puppy, Rufus. They were the size of full-grown beagles – but much more leggy and gawky.

Like Rufus, the pups were bright-eyed, strong and playful. Seeing the pups made Stella feel proud. She wasn't the type to brag, but she knew the pups would have died without her.

Last month, someone had shot Juliet's mate, Romeo. The Park Service people knew that raising eight pups was too much work for one wolf. They'd decided to bring Juliet and the pups back to the pen, where they could help Juliet raise her young.

Norma and Mack had captured Juliet without any problems. But when they went back to pick up the pups, they were gone. Juliet had moved them. Stella and her best friend, Josie, had climbed a mountain and searched until they found the pups.

Thinking of Romeo dead made Stella's chest feel hollow and achy. He had been beautiful – dark grey, huge, majestic, with an intelligent light in his eyes.

A local man had shot him: Lincoln Tyler. Stella knew him by sight. She'd seen him in the grocery store a couple of times. He worked at a lumber mill.

Norma said he could be fined a hundred thousand dollars. He might even go to jail for a year. But the thought of Lincoln Tyler getting punished didn't make Stella feel better. Jail time and fines wouldn't change the fact that Romeo was dead.

Norma and Mack locked up the pen. The threesome started hiking back towards the road. They moved slowly because of the heat. The temperature was hovering around ninety degrees – about ten degrees hotter than it should be in Montana in July. The heat made Stella feel like cooked spaghetti.

As they walked through the lodgepole pine forest, Stella was thinking about the coming weekend. It was the Fourth of July, and her home town of Gateway was hosting a rodeo. Stella had an important job to do. She was going to help her Aunt

Anya with any animal emergencies that came up.

Anya was Gateway's only vet. She took care of the ranchers' cattle and sheep. She fixed up cats, dogs, horses and goats. Sometimes she even tended wild creatures like raccoons and falcons. This weekend, she was also going to be the rodeo's official vet.

Stella wanted to be a vet when she grew up, so she spent as much time as possible with her aunt. Stella had been thrilled when Anya had asked her to help out at the rodeo.

Back at the trailhead, Norma and Stella said goodbye to Mack. Then they climbed into Norma's truck.

"Look at this traffic," Norma said a few minutes later. She'd just made the turn onto one of Goldenrock's main roads. It was packed full of 4 × 4s, RVs, luxury sedans, and compact cars lined up bumper to bumper. Creeping forward.

Most of the licence plates were from out of town. The national park was always crowded on holiday weekends. But because of the rodeo, July the Fourth was the busiest.

Stella didn't mind the traffic. A longer trip meant more time in the truck's air-conditioning. Beside, the view out of her window was outstanding. She could see a big swatch of blue sky. In the middle distance was a rocky mountain range. A little closer was a hill covered with pine trees. Closer still was an open pasture.

A couple of dozen buffalo were grazing the brown knee-high grass near the pasture's edge. They seemed unaware of the stream of motorists gawking at them.

"Buffalo are so amazing," Stella murmured.

Norma didn't answer. She was fiddling with the radio.

Even at this distance, Stella thought, the buffalo looked freakishly big. There was something ancient about their oversized heads and shaggy-rug fur. They were like Neanderthal cows. One look and you knew their species had been roaming the earth for a good long time.

Suddenly Stella sat up straighter. "Hey Mom – what's that man doing?"

A tourist – he had to be a tourist – was ambling across the pasture towards the buffalo. He was a big man, one hundred and thirty-five kilograms at least. Maroon shorts. Matching shirt. Blue baseball cap. He had a dog on a leash, a big bulldog that swaggered along at his side, looking like a four-legged muscleman. In his other hand was a large video camera.

Norma groaned. "I think he's looking for a photo opportunity."

"What should we do?"

Buffalo aren't especially dangerous. But they sometimes get annoyed if people get too close. Making a home movie with a wild animal is never a good idea.

"We'll tell him it's a bad idea," Norma said. "Just as soon as I can get out of this traffic. Come on, Mr Arizona – move it!"

In front of them was a lime-green Beetle, one of the new ones. It had an Arizona sunset-over-the-desert licence plate. Only a few inches separated Norma's front bumper and the Beetle's back bumper. Norma couldn't pull to the left. There was a line of oncoming traffic there. She couldn't pull to the right either. The shoulder on the side of the road was narrow and bounded by a deep ditch.

"Mom – beep at them." Stella turned back towards the pasture. "That man is getting way too close to the buffalo."

"Oh, OK . . ." Norma gave the horn a teeny blast. She hated loud noises – especially in the park, where people were supposed to be enjoying the sounds of nature.

Two people in the Beetle turned around to stare. Then they faced the front again. They still didn't move forward. Apparently the problem was farther up the line of cars.

"Let me get out," Stella said urgently. "I'll go and warn him."

"No," Norma said. "Those buffalo weigh over nine hundred kilograms. One of them could toss you all the way to Detroit."

"I won't get that close."

Norma leaned over to get a better view of the tourist. He was now a football field away from them – and closer to the buffalo. "What a dummy," she muttered.

"You have to let me get out, or let me drive the car," Stella insisted.

"OK – get out."

Stella didn't give Norma time to reconsider. She unsnapped her seat belt, pushed open the car door, and hopped out into the hot afternoon sun.

Two steps took her to the side of the drainage ditch. The ditch was waist-high. Dry, light-brown grass grew out of the bottom and sides. Stella thought she might be able to clear the ditch if she could get up some speed.

She began to run parallel to the road. Past the lime-green Beetle. Past a wheezing motor home. Now she could see what was slowing the traffic. The cars were edging around a maroon Buick that wasn't quite pulled out of the lane. It had to belong to the buffalo-loving tourist.

Stella ran another couple of yards and veered off towards the ditch. Right, left, right – and jump. She stretched her right leg out, out, out –

and came down on the other side of the ditch with two inches to spare.

"Ugh," she groaned. The momentum from her jump pitched her forward onto her hands and knees. The dry grass dug into her skin.

Oh, well. No time to worry about that now.

Stella jumped up. She started to run through the knee-high grass. "Mister. Hey – mister! Wait!"

The tourist didn't seem to hear. He kept ambling towards the band of buffalo with his dog trotting obediently at his side.

"Mister – stop!" *He must be daydreaming,*

Stella thought. *Or wearing headphones. Oh, no –* Stella stopped in her tracks.

Her eyes were focused on a buffalo near the edge of the band. She was still fifty yards back. But she knew what it meant when a bull lowered his head like that.

"Get out of the way!" Stella yelled.

The buffalo started to plod towards the tourist. He was like a freight train slowly getting up to speed.

Chug . . . ga . . . Chug . . . ga.

The buffalo picked up speed. Now he was trotting.

Chugga – chugga – chugga.

Now the buffalo was doing a stiff-legged canter.

Chugga chugga chugga.

Nine hundred kilograms was about the weight of a Volvo station wagon. Stella's animal encyclopaedia said buffalo could run forty miles an hour. She didn't think this one was moving that fast. Maybe more like twenty-five miles an hour. Twenty-five miles an hour straight towards the tourist and the bulldog. As fast as a freight train pulling out of the station.

Chuggachuggachugga.

Now the tourist saw the buffalo. He stopped. Reversed gears. Started to back up. Quickly.

The buffalo was really rolling now. Running. He plowed straight into the tourist's belly and tossed his head.

The tourist flew through the air like a rag doll. He was a good six feet up.

And the poor bulldog . . . he was airborne too! Yanked off his feet by the choke collar the tourist was still gripping in his pudgy hand.

❧ **2** ❧

The tourist landed hard on his backside. His head jerked back and hit the ground.

"Ow," Stella whispered.

The bulldog hit the ground a second later. He landed on his side, scrambled to his feet, and let out a puzzled bark. He stood staring down at his owner.

Stella listened to her heart beat. The tourist was lying still. Not moving. Wait . . . now he was sitting up! Stella let out her breath. She was relieved the fall hadn't knocked him unconscious.

Now the tourist caught sight of the buffalo – which wasn't more than two metres away from him. He hopped to his feet with surprising speed. He did a 180 turn and came barrelling back towards the road. He still had the dog's lead gripped tightly in one hand. The bulldog was doing his best to keep up, but he was struggling.

The buffalo followed along for about ten metres. Then he lost interest and slowed to a walk.

Stella ran to intercept the man. "Hey – mister!"

The tourist's head snapped towards her. Then he turned back towards the road and kept running. Stella went after him. Catching up wasn't difficult. He wasn't moving very fast.

"Little girl," the fat man huffed. His face was red and he was fighting for each breath. "Get out . . . of here . . . fast! One of those buffalo . . . is crazy! It attacked me!"

Stella put a hand on the man's elbow. They were moving along at a half jog. "That's because you got too close," she explained.

The man glanced nervously over his shoulder. "This is . . . probably . . . too close . . . too."

"Wait!" Stella reached out and grabbed his arm. "You're OK now. Look." She pointed towards the band of buffalo. The animal that had attacked the tourist had blended back into the group. Stella wasn't even sure which one was the attacker.

The tourist stopped running and stared. "Well, I . . . can't believe it. I thought he . . . had it in for me."

"He was probably just protecting one of the band's calves," Stella explained. "Listen – are you all right?"

The tourist rubbed his backside and smiled ruefully. His face was bright red from exertion.

"Probably going to feel that fall tomorrow."

Stella chuckled. "Probably."

The tourist began to laugh too. He sounded slightly hysterical. "Hey – this is going to make a great story. All of my friends have been to Goldenrock. But none of them has been butted by a buffalo. Geez, I can see the expression in their eyes when I tell them . . ."

Stella tuned out the tourist. She knelt down to the bulldog's eye level. "Hey, big guy, what's your . . . whoa."

The bulldog wasn't acting the way a friendly dog acts when he meets someone new. No wagging tail. No happy pant.

He *was* panting. But each breath was a head-hanging, painful struggle. Just watching him made Stella feel short of breath. And something else . . . his face looked strange. Puffy. Maybe swollen. Stella felt a quick spurt of fear. She wasn't sure why. But this dog needed help.

"Mister, your dog is having a hard time breathing. He needs to see a vet right away."

"Vet?" The man's voice had gone all weird. He sounded . . . amazed. Stella looked up at him. He was staring off in the middle distance. Towards the road.

His attitude made Stella mad. How could this guy space out when his dog was in danger? "Yes,

14

a vet," she said sternly. "And when I said 'right away,' I meant now!"

"OK," the man said in the same dreamy tone.

Then he crumpled. Down onto his bottom. And then pretty much straight back. He hit his head again, and the impact shoved his baseball cap over his face.

"What the . . ." Stella breathed.

The bulldog was startled. He took a few steps back and stood staring at his owner.

"Oh, my God," Stella whispered. Obviously, something was terribly wrong with his man. Maybe he'd hit his head harder than he'd realized. Maybe he had concussion.

She dropped onto her knees next to him and gave his chubby arm a shake. "Mister . . . hey! Wake up."

Nothing.

Now what? Stella looked around frantically and was relieved to see her mother jogging towards her. "Stella – what happened?"

"He passed out!"

Norma pulled her mobile phone off her belt. She pushed a button. Stella could hear her yelling into the phone.

"We have an emergency! A man in need of an ambulance. Possible concussion. About a mile from the north entrance to the park. Left side of the road if you're heading south."

Norma reached them, skidded to a stop, and dropped to her knees on the other side of the man.

"The buffalo butted him," Stella said. "Then he was fine. We were talking. And then – bam! He collapsed."

"Shh . . ." Norma was taking his pulse, looking at her watch. "He's breathing OK . . ."

"Oh, Mom! The dog. Something's wrong with the dog too. He's having trouble breathing. And his face looks funny."

Norma nodded without taking her eyes off the man. "One thing at a time." She tapped on the man's shoulder. "Sir – can you hear me?"

No reply.

Stella cast a nervous look at the bulldog. He'd hunched down into a sit and was panting like he had just run up fifty flights of stairs. His face looked puffier. Did bulldogs always look that way? Stella didn't think so.

"Muffin, help me turn his guy onto his side," Norma said.

"Mom, that's impossible. He's huge!"

"And if he throws up he's going to be dead. Now, come on, get into position."

Stella crawled around so that she and Norma were both on the other side of the man.

"On three," Norma said. "One, two, three."

Norma pushed the man's shoulder. Stella worked on his hip. It felt like pushing into soft dough. And it wasn't working. The guy had to weigh 110 kilograms. But then . . . slowly . . . he tipped onto his side.

"Good work," Norma said.

"Thanks." Stella sat back on her heels and brushed the sweat out of her eyes. She could hear sirens in the distance.

The ambulance must have been travelling in the other lane because Stella couldn't see it. She did see the line of cars on the road part slightly. Two uniformed paramedics came through the opening. They crashed straight through the drainage ditch and trotted towards them.

Norma and Stella scooted out of the way as the two men swiftly went to work.

One had flat Native American features and a long black ponytail. He pulled a small vial out of his shirt pocket, uncapped it, and waved it under the fat man's nose.

"Smelling salts," he explained when he saw Stella staring.

"What are smelling salts?"

He laughed. "Salts that *smell*. Bad enough to wake you up from the deepest sleep."

The fat man's nose wrinkled. He turned away from the vial, opened his eyes, and tried to sit up.

"Where's Rocky?" he demanded.

"Whoa, mister – hang on," the other paramedic said. He was older with thinning grey hair and glasses. "Let us check you out first."

"Where's Rocky?"

Rocky had to be the dog. "He's right here." Stella said. "He's . . . OK, I guess." The truth was Rocky didn't look that good. He was still panting. Still puffy. And his eyes seemed strange. Empty. Like he had turned his attention inside.

The paramedics were doing their thing. Temperature. Pressure. Examining the man's eyes.

"You have concussion," the paramedic with the

ponytail said gently. "You need to go to the hospital for some tests."

"Can Rocky go with me?"

"Sorry, man, that's impossible. It's against the rules to have a dog in the ambulance."

"Break the rules," the man begged. "Please."

"There's no point," the second paramedic explained. "The nurses would never admit you with a dog."

"But I can't leave him." The man sounded determined. "If Rocky can't go to the hospital, I'm not going either."

The paramedics exchanged looks.

"We can call one of your friends," the one with the ponytail offered. "Have them pick up the dog."

The man shook his head firmly. "I'm here on business. My closest friend is five hundred miles away."

Norma spoke up. "We can take care of Rocky," she said soothingly. "My sister is the vet here in town. She can board Rocky until you're able to pick him up."

The ponytailed paramedic gave Norma a big friendly smile. "You're Anya's sister? Yes! Now I see the resemblance. Great lady, Anya. Great vet, too. She gave my dog all her shots."

"She's my aunt," Stella said proudly.

"Rocky doesn't like kennels," the fat man said stubbornly.

"Oh, man, send the dog to Anya," the paramedic insisted. "He'll be in good hands."

"And it's not like a normal kennel," Stella said. "We walk the dogs ourselves. Outside. We even take them to the park."

The fat man considered. Then he lifted his head and motioned for Stella to come closer. "I'll let Rocky go to your aunt's clinic. But only if you promise not to let anyone but your aunt near him."

"OK," Stella shrugged.

"And don't take him to the park."

"All right."

"Promise?"

"Sure."

Stella figured the concussion was making the man act funny. Why else wouldn't he want his dog taken to the park?

The paramedics got him onto the stretcher. They picked him up and started back towards the ambulance, practically staggering under the load. Norma and Stella watched them for a moment.

"How are they going to get over the drainage ditch?" Norma wondered. She started to jog towards them. "Hey . . . guys. Let me help you. That ditch is pretty deep."

Stella picked up Rocky's lead. "Come on, boy. We have to take you to the doctor too." She pulled gently on the leash and took a few steps.

Rocky didn't follow. He had his head down. Every breath was a ragged gasp.

❖ 3 ❖

Stella didn't know what to do. Her mother was busy helping the paramedics carry the stretcher over the ditch. They definitely had their hands full. Very full. Maybe Rocky was just being stubborn. Maybe she should pull on his collar. But that couldn't be a good thing for a dog that was having trouble breathing.

There was only one solution . . .

Stella knelt down and slipped both arms under Rocky's low-slung belly. Then she forced her knees to straighten. She felt the strain in her legs, her back and her arms. Rocky was heavy. The effort of picking him up made Stella gasp.

But Rocky was gazing at her with fear in his dark eyes. Stella had to get him to the clinic. Something told her that she didn't have ten minutes to wait for her mother to come back and help.

She headed towards the road. It wasn't that far – maybe fifty metres. But every step was a struggle. Rocky's weight seemed to press her feet into the dry ground.

Stella was most of the way there when Norma came back to see what was keeping her. "Muffin – what are you doing? That dog must weigh twenty kilograms!"

"He can't walk. He can't breathe."

Norma lifted Rocky out of Stella's arms. The pattern of his fur was pressed into Stella's sweaty skin. She rubbed her forearms, getting the blood moving again.

"He *is* having a hard time," Norma said. "Well, Mr Naylor is on his way to hospital. Now it's Rocky's turn."

The ride into town passed in a blur. Stella sat in the back seat holding Rocky on her lap. She was only dimly aware of the passing scenery and the call Norma made to Anya. She had her eyes on Rocky. She wanted to be sure he kept breathing.

Anya was waiting for them on the pavement outside the clinic. She opened the door and peeked in at Rocky.

"He can hardly breathe," Stella said.

"Getting worse?"

"Yes."

Anya shook her head, looking concerned. "Sounds like a tear in his windpipe." She began to work her arms under the dog's belly.

"How would his windpipe tear?" Stella wiggled around towards the open door so it would be easier for Anya to pick up Rocky.

"He's wearing a choke collar," Anya said. She grunted as she lifted the dog. "What happened when his owner was thrown?"

"Rocky was yanked right off his feet."

"That could do it." Anya turned towards the clinic, heading up the steps at a fast pace.

Stella looked at Norma, who was twisted around in the front seat. "Are you coming in?"

Norma glanced at her watch. "Can't, I'm ten minutes late to pick up Cora. I promised to buy her a new hat for tomorrow. I'll see you at home."

"Great!" Stella jumped out of the car, slammed the door, and ran after Anya. Up the three steps to the porch. In the door. Down the hall.

Anya's basset hound, Boris, came out of the office to greet Stella. *Click, Click, Click*. His toenails tapped on the vinyl floor. He gave her a look that seemed to say, "What's going on *now*?"

"Don't worry, everything's fine." Stella paused long enough to scratch behind Boris's long, hanging ears. Then she hurried into the operating room. Anya was standing at the table, examining Rocky's throat.

Rocky was sitting limply on the stainless steel table. Anya had removed his collar, but he was still struggling for air. Each intake of breath was quivery, uncertain. Each breath came out in puffs.

As awful as his breathing sounded, Rocky looked more mellow. The panic had drained out of his droopy eyes. He was blinking sleepily. He yawned, stretching out his massive chops, and then settled them in place. Stella guessed that Anya had given him a sedative.

"This is unusual," Anya said.

"What?" Stella asked.

"The dog—"

"Rocky?" Stella interrupted.

Anya nodded vaguely. "Rocky's face is filling up with air." A note of wonder had crept into her voice.

"Air? Are you sure his face isn't just swollen?"

"It's not swollen," Anya said. "I can tell by the feel. His skin feels . . . crinkly. Like a paper bag."

"Where is the air coming from?"

"Leaking out of his windpipe."

"Is he going to die?"

Anya laughed. "No, he'll be fine. Let's watch him for an hour. Then, if his condition hasn't improved, I'll operate."

An hour passed. Rocky's face didn't look any different and he wasn't breathing any easier. Anya decided to operate. Stella felt itchy. She was trying to decide whether she should stay in the operating room or make herself busy elsewhere in the clinic.

She'd watched her aunt operate a few times. Before the operation began, she always felt nervous. Sweaty. Something about seeing an animal cut open, seeing what skin and muscles usually hid, was creepy.

And fascinating. Once the operation began, Stella always forgot about her moist palms, her queasy stomach, her knocking knees. Watching Anya put things right somewhere deep inside an animal was amazing.

And there was so much to learn. Stuff Stella planned to use when she grew up and became a vet.

"Can you help me with the straps?" Anya asked.

"Sure."

Rocky was sound asleep now. Stella and Anya gently laid him on his back and strapped him to the table. Anya positioned the dog's head so that his neck was exposed. She shaved the incision site with an electric razor and disinfected it.

Stella felt like the time to leave had passed. Besides, she felt responsible for Rocky. After all, his owner was in the hospital. Someone should watch over the dog.

The operation went quickly. Anya exposed

Rocky's windpipe by cutting through the skin and thin muscle that covered it. The windpipe looked like a vacuum hose, only skinnier. It was a straw-like tube with evenly spaced reinforcing rings that looked like cartilage.

"I see the tear," Anya announced. "Right here in his throat. Good thing too. I didn't want to have to open his chest cavity."

"Yeah . . . good." Stella felt a bit faint. Open his chest cavity? That didn't sound pretty.

"Want to see?"

"Sure."

Anya used an instrument to point out a half-inch opening in Rocky's windpipe. The tear didn't look big enough to cause so much trouble.

"Hmmm . . . tissue looks fine," Anya said. "This is just going to take a few sutures."

Stella watched as her aunt used a needle and thread to stitch up the small tear. Then Anya sewed the muscle and skin back together and bandaged the incision.

"That wasn't so bad," Stella said.

Anya flashed her a smile. "No. Now we just need to keep an eye on him for a few days."

Stella and Anya were back in the boarder room, getting Rocky settled, when someone knocked at the front door.

"I'll get it!" Stella ran down the hallway. She

was ready for the next emergency. So she was surprised when she opened the door and found Marisa Capra and Josie Russell on the stoop. Josie was smiling, but Marisa had an uneasy look on her face. She was hanging back a bit.

"What are you guys doing here?"

"We have a meeting, remember?"

It took a moment for Stella's mind to click into gear. Then she did remember. Right. The rodeo meeting. But that wasn't supposed to be until five. She stepped out of the doorway.

"What time is it?"

"A little after five. Sorry we're late."

Stella smiled to herself. OK, so maybe the operation hadn't been that fast. Rocky had been in the operating room for more than an hour and a half.

"Sit down," Stella said. "I'll get Anya."

But Anya was already coming into the waiting room. She was carrying a cardboard box. "Hey, Josie, Marisa. Thanks for agreeing to help out this weekend."

"You're welcome. What's in the box?" Josie asked eagerly.

"Cool stuff!" Anya sat the box on the floor and began struggling with the flaps.

Stella could feel waves of excitement coming off Josie and Anya. Rodeo fever. The Gateway Rodeo was the biggest event of the summer. People got just as keyed up for the rodeo as they did for Christmas. Stella glanced at Marisa, expecting to see her smiling.

Marisa looked about as happy as a duck in the desert. Stella wanted to ask her what was wrong. But she was distracted when Anya pulled out a fire-engine-red T-shirt and said, "Ta da!"

The shirt said GOODWIN VETERINARY SERVICES across the front in bold white letters. Goodwin was Anya's last name.

"Cool," Josie said.

"I got one for each of you," Anya said, sounding proud. She pulled the shirts out of the box and tossed them at the girls.

Stella caught hers and pulled it on.

"And this is the really great part," Anya said. "Walkie-talkies!" She pulled devices out of the box. "During the rodeo, we can all keep in touch with these."

She started to hand them out. One for Stella. One for Josie. But when Anya held the walkie-talkie out to Marisa, Marisa shook her head and refused to take it.

"What's wrong?" Anya asked.

"I have to tell you something." Marisa's voice was a whisper. "I . . . I can't help out at the rodeo."

29

"Why not?" Anya asked.

Now Marisa looked up. Her eyes were bright with anger. "I know what happens at rodeos."

"What happens?" A note of caution had crept into Anya's tone.

"Animals are mistreated," Marisa said. "Bulls are tortured. They get their ribs broken and the cowboys put barbed wire—"

Josie groaned loudly. "Who told you *that*?"

Marisa spun around to face her. "My mother."

Josie groaned again. "I should have known."

"Girls," Anya tried.

"What's that supposed to mean?" Marisa demanded. She had a red blotch on each cheek.

Josie held up a finger. "One question. Just one. Has your mother ever been to a rodeo?"

"No, she boycotts them."

"Then how does she know the animals are mistreated?"

"She read it."

"Read it where?"

"On the internet."

"Girls," Anya tried again.

"Well, that's nice," Josie said. "But did she ever think to ask someone who has been to rodeos? Did she ever think it might be a good idea to go see for herself?"

"Girls!" Anya was getting to her feet. Getting to her feet and holding out a hand. Smiling.

Stella spun around. A man was standing in the doorway. Or a boy. Or something in between. He was skinny. His pants bagged down around his hips. His thin, blond bangs covered his eyes.

"Are you Travis?" Anya smiled.

The boy smiled and nodded.

Anya stood near him, looking protective. "Girls – this is Travis. He's a student at Montana State and he'd going to help out at the clinic on weekends."

"Hi, Travis," Stella said.

Marisa and Josie had already turned back to their argument.

31

"She doesn't go to rodeos because that would just make people who abuse animals rich," Marisa said.

"Maybe she's scared of finding out she's wrong," Josie said.

They were like two dogs fighting over a bone.

"I'll need to show Travis around," Anya said. "Josie, I'll pick you up tomorrow at seven-thirty. Marisa, let me know what you decide."

Stella watched Anya lead Travis down to her office. She felt a little funny. She was Anya's helper. Why did her aunt need Travis?

"Stella . . . tell her," Josie insisted.

"Marisa, I've been to bunches of rodeos," Stella said. "I've never seen any animal hurt. Do you think Anya would let that happen?"

"I just think rodeos are mean," Marisa insisted. "I'm boycotting. And I think you guys should too."

Josie looked at Stella, a pleading look in her eyes.

"I'm going," Stella said. "I promised Anya." She felt sort of surprised. When it came to animal issues, she usually agreed with Marisa – not Josie.

"Good," Josie said.

Marisa shrugged and started to get up. "I've got to go," she said. "I have to help Mom get dinner ready." Marisa's family ran a bed-and-breakfast,

32

a cosy kind of inn. Marisa helped with the cooking and cleaning sometimes.

Josie hung around after Marisa left. "We should get someone to take her place."

"What about Amanda?" Amanda Foster had been in the girls' class the year before.

"She's on vacation. In France."

"Wow. Well . . . how about Jared?"

Josie shrugged. "Fine with me."

Stella looked up Jared's number in the phone book. He answered on the first ring and immediately agreed to help.

4

Stella got up the next morning at six-thirty. She padded downstairs in her bare feet and found her entire family in the kitchen.

Cora was pawing through a cabinet, looking for something. Jack was at the stove. Norma was sitting at the table in her green Parks Department uniform. A steaming cup of coffee sat in front of her. She was plunking ice cubes into it. Even this early, the morning was already hot.

"Morning," Stella said.

"How many pancakes can you eat?" Jack asked.

"I don't know," Stella said. She sat down in the doorway and pulled Rufus onto her lap. He licked her nose and wagged his tail. "Maybe three?"

"Mom, have you seen the purple shoe polish?"

Norma yawned. "I'm not even sure they make purple shoe polish."

"Mom! I had some for my good boots."

"Then I'm sure it's in the cabinet."

"Cora, sit down," Jack said. "Your pancakes

are ready. You too Stella."

"I can't eat," Cora said. "I'm too nervous."

"Just try."

Stella slipped into her usual chair. So did Cora. Stella took a sip of the juice her father had put on the table. She put some butter on her pancakes, and added the perfect amount of syrup.

Cora didn't move. She just stared down at her food. "Dad . . . I can't."

"Oh, OK."

Stella smiled at her sister. She knew what a big day it was for her. The barrel racing competition was later that afternoon. Cora had been training for it all summer.

"Do you think Cinnamon is nervous?" Stella asked.

"I hope not," Cora said. "And if she can tell how nervous I am, we're toast."

Cinnamon was a six-year-old Quarter horse. She belonged to Jake Romulo. He owned Jake's Stables, where Cora worked. Cora was a guide who led city folks on horseback rides of Goldenrock. She was also a stable hand – mucking out stalls, hauling in fresh hay.

Jake was a generous man, and he let Cora ride Cinnamon as often as she liked. Cinnamon wasn't one of the trail horses. She was a barrel horse, specifically trained for barrel racing. Cinnamon had heart. She was fast and fearless on the turns, but she was still learning her game. Still figuring how to cope with the pressure of competition.

"I don't know why I'm so nervous," Cora said. "I'm not expecting to win."

"Well, you never know," Jack said.

"Dad, I know. Tara Tyler Smith, remember? Her best time is two seconds faster than mine."

Tara Tyler Smith was the national barrel racing champion. Stella had read an article about her in *American Girl* magazine. Tara was a real cowgirl. Her father had given her a small herd of cattle when she was ten. Rumour had it that she rode rough stock – wild horses – on her father's ranch in Texas.

"Are you scared about getting up in front of all those people?" Norma asked. About five hundred people usually showed up for barrel racing events. Barrel racing was one of the most popular parts of the rodeo.

"No," Cora said. "I don't really get stage fright. Maybe I'm not nervous at all. Maybe I'm just excited. I can't wait to see Annie Oakley."

"Kind of late for that," Jack said. "She died about seventy years ago."

"Not that Annie Oakley," Cora said. "Annie Oakley is Tara's horse."

"Ah. So our champion knows her rodeo history," Jack said. "I approve."

"Good," Cora said. "But don't forget you're supposed to cheer for me."

"I will," Jack promised.

"Me too," Stella said. "What time is the race?"

"Three o'clock sharp."

A little while later, Cora left for the stable. Anya arrived to pick up Stella. They drove out to get Josie and then headed back to town.

"Where does Jared live?" Josie asked.

"Just out of town," Anya said. "On Route 202."

Stella had never been to Jared's house before, so she looked around with interest when Anya turned into the Frye's driveway.

"Lawn could use some work," Josie said.

"Driveway too," Anya said.

The grass in the yard had gone to seed. There were no neat flower beds. No pruned scrubs, just grass that sorely needed a mow. The ruts in the driveway were deep enough to send Anya's 4×4 bouncing.

The house was a wooden A-frame. Jared was waiting on the low-slung porch. He saw them and started down the porch steps.

"Thanks for inviting me," Jared said shyly as he climbed into the truck.

"Thanks for agreeing to help," Anya said.

Everyone was quiet as Anya backed the truck onto the grass and turned it around.

"What have you been doing this summer?" Josie asked Jared.

"Reading."

Another pause. Then Stella handed Jared his GOODWIN VETERINARY SERVICES T-shirt. He smiled and took it.

"So where is the rodeo?" Jared asked.

Josie stared at him like he'd just asked what planet they were on. "You don't know where the rodeo is? Where have you been? Hiding under a rock?"

"I told you . . . reading."

"Well, try reading the newspaper sometime!" Josie exclaimed.

"Town fairgrounds," Stella said.

"Where are the—" Jared started.

"Practically right in the middle of town!" Josie shouted. "Three blocks from City Hall. Five minutes from your house. Didn't you see them put up the Ferris wheel?"

"Um . . . no."

"Don't tell me you've never been to a rodeo before!"

Jared gave Stella a helpless shrug. "Is that a problem?"

"Of course not," Stella said.

Josie still looked annoyed. "Where are you from, anyway?"

"Ohio."

"Sound like Ohio is a pretty poor place."

Jared shrugged. "I guess. If you're looking for a rodeo, anyway."

That shut Josie up until they got to the fairground. It wasn't much past eight. But the car park was already half full. Acres and acres of cars and trucks were baking in the morning sunshine.

Knots of people moved from their trucks and cars towards the main gate. The gate was surrounded by balloons. A banner read WELCOME TO THE ANNUAL GATEWAY RODEO! A few people were unloading horse trailers. Stella looked for Cora, but didn't see her.

Anya pulled into a space marked Staff Parking Only. Everyone climbed out the truck. Jared pulled off the T-shirt he was wearing and put on his GOODWIN VETERINARY SERVICES shirt. Anya explained how to use the walkie-talkies. She showed them how the walkie-talkies attached to their belts.

"The announcer will tell people to look for kids in red shirts if they have an animal emergency," Anya reminded them. "If someone comes to you with an emergency, call me right away."

Josie nodded.

"OK," Stella said.

"What's that smell?" Jared demanded.

Anya led the way to a special staff entrance. A man waved them through. They emerged at one end of the fairway. Booths stretched out as far as Stella could see. Most of them were just opening.

Some of the booths had games. Shooting galleries. Ping-pong ball tosses. Fortune-tellers.

Some had food. Candyfloss. Sausages and peppers. Hot dogs. Candied apples.

Small knots of people were gathered in front of some booths. Other people were strolling down the fairway, looking this way and that, taking in the scene.

Anya glanced at her watch. "I'm late to check on the stock. Better go."

"What do you want us to do?" Jared asked.

"Have fun. And call me if you need me." Anya gave them a smile and a wave, and walked off towards the main barn.

Stella turned to the others. "What should we do first?"

Jared took a deep breath. "Eat some of whatever I'm smelling."

Josie stuck her nose in the air and sniffed. "Waffles." She smiled at Jared for the first time. "Let's go. They usually set up the booth near the horse barn. Far end of the fairway."

"Waffles?" Jared looked confused.

"Not the kind you eat at breakfast," Stella explained. "A special kind you can only get at the rodeo. They're thicker than homemade waffles. And crispier. And they put powdered—"

"What's happening up there?" Josie interrupted.

Stella stared down the fairway. People were acting strangely, but she couldn't see why. A girl wearing a pink sundress screamed and grabbed her father's arm. A baby suddenly started wailing. A woman with long, blonde hair was pointing at something.

Stella stood on her tiptoes, straining to see what was happening. She saw a sheepdog bounding towards her down the fairway. He was a big dog, light tan and friendly-looking. So what was the big deal?

"Look at that!" Josie said.

Stella glanced at her friend. She saw that Josie wasn't looking at the dog. Her gaze was higher. Stella looked in the same direction. And she saw the strangest sight! It was some sort of small creature – a monkey! – dressed like a miniature cowboy. It was as if an illustration from a *Curious George* book had suddenly come to life – because this monkey was completely, totally alive.

He leaped from one red-and-white booth canopy to the next. All the while, he was letting out an ear-piercing call.

"Oooo-HA-HA-HA!"

The monkey reached a booth without a canopy and veered into the crowd. He leaped off a man's shoulder and landed on a woman's head.

"Oooo-HA-HA-HA!"

The woman batted frantically at her hair. "Norman, help! Get him off me!"

Norman made a grab for the monkey, but he was too late.

Now Stella understood why the crowd was scattering. No one wanted to be a springboard for this crazy monkey.

The monkey pushed off from the woman's head and landed on a canopy on the other side

of the fairway.

"Oooo-HA-HA-HA!"

The animals kept coming closer. First the big furry sheepdog. Then the crazed, laughing monkey.

"Now *this* is what I call an animal emergency," Jared said, sounding happy. He was enjoying the chaos.

The sheepdog was close enough now that Stella could see he was wearing a pink collar.

Stella stepped out in the middle of the now-empty fairway. The crowd had scattered to the sides.

The dog was heading straight for her.

Stella raised one hand. "Sit!" she commanded.

She said it just right, exactly the way Zack, the instructor at Rufus's obedience class, had taught her. A firm, I'm-not-joking tone.

She didn't expect it to work. Whenever Stella tried it on Rufus, he just wagged his tail and licked her hand.

The sheepdog had a completely different reaction. He immediately stopped running. He skidded to a stop right in front of Stella and put his backside down on the pavement.

"Wow," Stella said.

But what happened next actually made the crowd gasp. The monkey cowboy swung off a nearby canopy, dropped onto the dog's back, and straddled him like a horse!

Stella stared down at their two little faces.

They stared back at her – apparently waiting for her next order.

❖ 5 ❖

Josie moved smoothly around Stella's side. She reached out and grabbed the monkey's collar.

Stella reached for the dog's.

The girls looked at each other. Now what?

"Tiny! Tiny . . . hey, did anyone see a monkey?" The voice came from down the fairway.

Stella turned in that direction. She saw a woman pointing out the animals to a man. He was wearing a shirt with blue and pink polka dots, denim overalls at least three sizes too big, yellow running shoes, and a bright red cowboy hat. His eyes were circled with black greasepaint. But the circles were only half filled in.

The crowd parted as the clown hurried up to them. He snapped leads on the dog and monkey. "Tiny, are you troubling these young ladies?"

The monkey hung his head.

"Well, you should be ashamed!" The clown took Stella's hand and kissed it. Then he kissed Josie's hand. "My name is Red Patches," he said. "Thank you very much for catching my gallivanting pets. Tiny got away from me. Then he unleashed Horse – and the race was on."

"Has this happened before?" Jared asked.

"More times than I can count." Red Patches gave Stella and Josie a broad wink. "Of course, I can only count to ten."

Josie rolled her eyes, but Stella laughed.

"I don't know what I would have done if you hadn't caught them," Red said.

"No problem," Stella said. She pointed to her T-shirt. "We're here to deal with animal emergencies."

"You look a little young to be a vet."

"I'm not a vet. But my aunt is."

"Oh." Red looked thoughtful. "You know," he said, "I have a bunny who needs a vet."

Stella was instantly more alert. "What's wrong with her?"

"Her appetite is off. And" – Red Patches leaned closer and lowered his voice – "And she hasn't . . . er, relieved herself in several days."

The clown's expression darkened. "Miss Piggy has been with me for eight years. I'd hate to lose her."

"Your bunny's name is Miss Piggy?" Jared asked.

Now the clown looked surprised. "You've never heard of her?"

Jared looked at Stella for help. "Well, I . . ."

Stella had never heard of Miss Piggy either. But she guessed the rabbit was part of Red's act.

"This is his first rodeo," Stella explained.

Red Patches's expression brightened. "Well, that explains it, then!" Red started down the fairway, leading Horse and Tiny. Stella, Josie and Jared followed.

"See, what happens is that my partner, Buckaroo Bob, walks into the arena and faints," Red continued. "I drive an ambulance into the area, hop out, and give Bob a quick examination."

Red was leading them back towards the car park. He didn't seem to mind when Tiny crawled up his leg and sat down on his shoulder. "I announce my diagnosis, loud enough so that they can hear me in the next county. 'It's an ingrown hair!' Then I pull Miss Piggy out of Buckaroo Bob's shirt."

Josie shot Stella a puzzled look.

Red noticed. "Hair, hare – get it? Hair like on your head and hare like Miss Piggy."

Stella smiled and nodded. "That's a pretty silly joke."

"Silly jokes are the best kind!" Red exclaimed.

47

They had reached a grassy field out by the parking lot. About a dozen RVs were parked there. Red pointed to one of them. "Home, sweet home."

Red's RV was one of the old-fashioned aluminium ones. Compared to the other vehicles, it was small and had rounded curves. It looked like a silver pumpkin on wheels.

A good-sized bunny hutch was sitting in the grass next to the trailer. Stella went up and looked in.

Miss Piggy was sitting in a cosy pile of hay. She was brown with a white underside. Her hind legs were powerful-looking. Her ears twitched nervously.

The rabbit's eyes were half closed. Stella thought she was panting slightly. And her fur was messy, as if someone had combed it the wrong way.

"What do you think?" Red asked.

Stella thought Miss Piggy looked pretty sick. But she didn't want to tell Red that. "I think my aunt should look at her," Stella said.

She took her walkie-talkie off her belt and pushed the rectangular call button. "Anya," she said into the microphone. "Come in."

"Hi, Stella." Anya's voice was a little difficult to hear over the static. "What's happening?"

Stella explained about Miss Piggy.

"I'll be right there."

Red glanced at his watch. "I'm on in ten minutes. I'd better finish my makeup."

"OK," Stella said. "We'll knock when Anya gets here."

Red clomped up three steps and disappeared into the trailer.

Stella sat down in the grass next to the cage to wait. She wanted a lemonade. It was hot.

Jared was staring off towards the fairway. They could hear music playing. They could smell hamburgers grilling.

"Hmm." Jared rubbed his belly. "Smells good."

"We never did get that waffle," Josie said.

"Why don't you guys go?" Stella suggested. "I'll wait for Anya."

"Are you sure?" Josie asked.

"Positive. You guys should be at the rodeo in case there's another emergency."

"That's true," Jared said.

"Call us on the walkie-talkie if you need us," Josie said.

Stella watched her friends go.

Anya appeared at the trailer a few minutes later. Red came out with his makeup finished. He watched as Anya examined Miss Piggy.

"When was the last time she pooped?" Anya asked.

Red sounded embarrassed. "Um . . . maybe the day before yesterday."

"Could be a fur ball," Anya said. "Rabbits get lots of those when they're shedding. They swallow fur while grooming their coats, just like cats. But unlike cats, they can't throw up the fur."

Stella watched as Anya twisted a latch and lifted one side of the cage away. She reached in to pick up Miss Piggy. Rabbits are usually nervous around people they don't know. Stella expected Miss Piggy to hide in her nesting box. But she didn't even attempt to hop away from Anya. Not a good sign.

Anya used one hand to grab Miss Piggy by the scruff of her neck. She scooped her other hand under the bunny's belly. She knelt down in the grass and put Miss Piggy down on her side. Now Miss Piggy started to squirm. She didn't like that. Red stood about three feet away. Even with his bright makeup on, Stella could tell that he was nervous.

"Stella, could you help hold her down?"

"Sure!" Stella knelt down next to Anya. "What do I do?"

"Hold her back legs in one hand and her front legs with the other."

Stella grabbed hold of Miss Piggy. She watched as Anya massaged the bunny's belly. "If she has a hair ball, I should be able to feel it."

"What does it feel like?" Stella asked.

"Like a thick mass . . ." Anya's expression was distant as she concentrated on what she was feeling. "Could be up to the size of a large marble."

"Can I feel?" Stella asked.

"Um . . . no." Anya looked puzzled. "There's nothing there. Not even a jelly bean-sized mass."

"Why not?"

"Miss Piggy doesn't have a fur ball."

"Then what's wrong with her?"

"Turn her over," Anya said.

Stella lifted Miss Piggy's legs, rolled her over, and exposed her other side. Anya gently pressed

51

down on Miss Piggy's side – just above where her legs joined her body.

Miss Piggy gave a terrific kick with her back legs.

"Whoa! I almost lost her there."

"Miss Piggy didn't like that," Anya said.

"What is it?" Red asked.

"Miss Piggy needs emergency surgery," Anya announced.

❧ 6 ❧

"What? Why?" Red demanded.

"Well, I'll have to do a blood test to be certain," Anya said calmly. "But I think Miss Piggy is having an appendicitis attack."

"Is she going to die?" Red demanded. He was hugging himself miserably. Stella felt awful for him. Miss Piggy was obviously an important part of his life.

"If it is her appendix, I can remove it," Anya said. "It's a serious condition. But she has a good chance."

Red suddenly rushed forwards and gave Anya an awkward hug. "Go. Do it," he said. "But take good care of her."

"We will," Anya promised with a faint smile. She asked Red for a shirt. He brought out one with red-and-white stripes.

Anya stuffed Miss Piggy into one sleeve. Her head poked out of the opening made for a hand. The tight-fitting garment calmed Miss Piggy.

"Stella, can you hold Miss Piggy in the truck?" Anya asked.

"No problem."

They said a rushed goodbye to Red and headed for Anya's 4 × 4 at a trot.

"I wish I had a siren," Anya muttered as she pulled into a line of cars slowly making its way out of the fairgrounds. She was drumming her fingers impatiently against the steering wheel.

"Is she that bad?" Stella asked.

"It's hard to say without blood tests," Anya said as she nosed the truck forwards into position for a right-hand turn. "But my guess is yes. And if that appendix ruptures, Miss Piggy is going to be one very sick bunny."

Five minutes later they pulled up in front of the clinic. Travis was in Anya's office. He tipped her desk chair back and watched them hurry in the front door. "What's up?"

"Emergency surgery," Anya said. "Why don't you help?"

"Me?" Travis pointed at himself.

"You're here to find out if you want to be a vet, right?" Anya said. "Might as well see what it's all about."

"Ah, what do I do?"

"Go in the operating room. Wash your hands. Suit up. Scrubs. One of those shower cap thingies over your hair. Mask."

Travis laughed uneasily. "Are you serious? All that for a bunny?"

Anya gave him a sharp look. "I'm serious."

"Oh . . . OK." Travis looked a bit pale as he stumbled down the hall and disappeared into the operating room. Stella heard the sink go on. She looked at the sick bunny in Anya's arms.

"Should I go back to the rodeo?" Stella asked.

"Sure," Anya said. "But could you walk Boris first?"

"You bet."

Stella peeked into the office. Boris was stretched out in his usual spot under the desk. "Come on, boy!" Stella said.

Boris gave her a baleful look.

Stella took Boris's lead off a hook on the back of the door. She rattled it. "Come on. Let's go." She smacked her palm against her thigh.

Boris hauled himself to his feet with a groan. He trotted out from under the desk and stood waiting for Stella to snap on his lead.

Stella laughed and patted him on his side. "Can't wait to get outside, huh?"

She led the dog down the back steps and waited while he peed in the backyard. Then she took him down the walkway to the pavement. Boris trotted along at her side, his long ears swaying

back and forth.

When they got back to the clinic, Stella got Boris some fresh water. While he lapped it up, she decided to check on Rocky.

He wasn't in his cage in the boarder room. At first Stella wasn't worried. Maybe Travis moved him. She went down the row, peeking in each cage. Except for one that contained a cat who was recuperating from an operation, all of the cages were empty.

Now Stella's heart was beating slightly faster than usual. Where was Rocky? She went back and checked the cages again. He definitely wasn't there.

Did Rocky get out of his cage somehow? Maybe Travis had let him out . . .

Stella decided to ask. She rushed down the hallway, but before she could go into the operating room, Travis burst out. He whipped off his surgical mask. He leaned against the hallway, panting. He had both arms wrapped around his belly.

"What's wrong?" Stella asked.

"Blood," Travis murmured. He looked like he was about to throw up.

"Oh," Stella said. Josie got the same way whenever she saw blood.

"Everything OK out there?" Anya called through the door.

"Yes!" Stella called back. "Need some help?"

"Nope. I'm just closing."

"Come on." Stella took Travis's arm and led him to the waiting room.

He came meekly.

"Sit down," she told him. "Put your head between your knees and take deep breaths."

Travis did as he was told.

Stella let him get in three good breaths. "Where's Rocky?" she demanded then.

"Who?" Travis still had his head between his legs. His voice was muffled.

"Rocky! The bulldog with a torn windpipe."

"Oh. His owner picked him up."

"But he wasn't ready to be released yet."

"I told her that. But she wouldn't take no for an answer. What was I supposed to do?"

"Explain that Rocky needed time to recover. Tell her—" Stella stopped, puzzled. "Wait a second. What do you mean 'she wouldn't take no for an answer'? Rocky's owner is a man. A fat man. Mr Naylor."

Travis sat up. He gave Stella a frightened look. "Rocky's owner is a woman. She had dark hair . . . sunglasses."

Stella was starting to feel sick herself. She remembered Mr Naylor saying his closest friend was five hundred miles away. She also remembered promising him that she'd watch over Rocky. She'd broken her promise. Big time.

She was still trying to figure out what to do when a knock came at the door. The doorbell rang. Then there was another knock.

Stella had a feeling she knew who was at the door. She got up and reluctantly opened it.

"I came for my dog," Mr Naylor said as he rolled into the room. "How's he doing?"

Stella and Travis exchanged glances.

"Um . . . I think you should talk to Anya," Travis said uneasily.

Mr Naylor's face fell. "Rocky isn't . . . dead, is he?"

58

"No . . ." Travis said. "At least, I don't think so."

Mr Naylor's face turned an alarming shade of red. "I demand to know what's going on with my dog!" he bellowed.

"Anya is in surgery," Travis said. "She should be finished soon."

Mr Naylor turned to Stella. "What happened? You promised not to let anyone touch him." Tears were standing in his eyes.

Stella swallowed hard. She didn't know how to tell Mr Naylor they'd lost his pet. He obviously cared a great deal about Rocky.

"Mr Naylor . . ." she started. "Well, someone came and picked up Rocky. A woman with sunglasses and dark hair."

Mr Naylor fell heavily into a chair. He slumped forward, looking utterly defeated. "Not again."

"Again?" Stella asked faintly.

"Rocky is always being dognapped." Mr Naylor's tone was matter-of-fact.

Stella looked at Travis. She could tell they were thinking the same thing. Maybe that buffalo had hit Mr Naylor harder than he realized. Maybe he belonged back in the hospital.

"Why would anyone want to steal your dog?" Travis asked delicately.

"Ever hear of the Bulldogs?" Mr Naylor's voice was resigned.

"No," Stella said.

"Well, sure," Travis said eagerly. "Farm-league baseball team out of Boulder. Wait . . . I bet Rocky is your mascot!"

"Bingo. Rival teams are always dognapping him. Trying to ruin the team's concentration before a big game."

"Does that work?"

"Sometimes." Mr Naylor sighed.

"Rocky is recovering from surgery," Stella said. "He needs rest. We should try to get him back somehow."

"How?" Travis asked.

"Well . . . maybe Assistant Sheriff Rose could help," Stella said.

And then . . .

"Err-ten-err" Stella's walkie-talkie began to squawk: first static, then Josie's voice. "Stella? Ten-four. This is Josie."

Stella pulled her walkie-talkie off her belt. She pushed the button and spoke into the microphone. "I read you, Josie. Go ahead."

"We need Anya in the practice arena right now. We've got a horse in serious trouble."

❧ 7 ❧

Anya had finished stitching up Miss Piggy. Stella helped her get the rabbit settled in the boarder room.

Leaving Travis to deal with Mr Naylor, they ran for Anya's truck. Anya drove through town as fast as she dared – motoring through an amber light and passing a creeping, crawling car full of gaping tourists. She parked right in front of the rodeo's main gate next to a sign that said *No Parking*.

Anya grabbed her horse bag out of the back and they ran through the crowds strolling down the fairway.

Josie was waiting for them just inside the gate to the practice arena. She wasn't one to panic easily, but her face was drawn with worry.

Jared was there too. He was hanging back as if he was afraid of getting in the way.

"Where's the horse?" Anya demanded.

"There."

Stella looked where Josie was pointing, and felt

her breath catch in her throat. The horse was a beautiful golden colour. A Palomino.

"Is that Annie Oakley?" Stella asked.

"Yup."

"What happened?" Anya asked as they started across the arena at a trot.

A couple of dozen people were gathered in the arena, watching the sick horse from a distance. Cora was there, standing with some of her friends. She was dressed for competition in dark trousers, purple boots, a pink embroidered blouse, and a new white cowboy hat. Everyone looked sober, like they were watching a tragedy unfold.

On the other side of the arena, a couple of women were exercising their horses. Tragedy was one thing, but the competition was still going on.

"Jared and I were watching the barrel racers warm up," Josie explained. "Tara Tyler Smith was putting Annie Oakley through her paces. Then something went wrong. Annie Oakley started to sweat and freak out. That's when I called you."

"Good work," Anya said.

The horse was in rough shape. As they approached, Stella could see that her hind legs kept buckling and then straightening out – as if she were struggling to stay on her feet.

A tiny girl had hold of Annie's reins. She had to

be Tara. She was petting the horse's nose and speaking softly to her. Her soothing words weren't having much effect, however.

Annie's eyes were wide with fear, showing the whites. She kept tossing her head and looking over her shoulder – as if she were afraid a ghost was sneaking up on her. Her coat was darkened with sweat.

Anya touched Tara's shoulder. "I'm the vet."

"Thank God you're here. Wh – what's wrong with her?"

"That's what I'm here to find out. I'm just going to take her pulse." Anya reached out and grabbed

the inside back of Annie's knee. She was quiet for ten seconds as she counted heartbeats.

"It's fast," Anya reported.

She went around the back of the animal and ran a hand lightly over her flank. Annie jumped away from her touch. "Her muscles are tense," Anya said.

"She's pretty nervous," Tara said.

Anya nodded. "Let me ask you some questions. Have you been exercising your horse in the same way as usual?"

"No," Tara admitted. "My family had to drive here from Texas. We couldn't go that fast with the trailer. We were on the road for two nights."

"Did you take Annie out of the trailer on the way?" Anya asked.

"Of course. We stayed with people who had pastures for Annie."

"And you rode her?"

"No. I had an allergy attack," Tara explained. "Cottonwood always makes me sneeze. Got so I could hardly see straight. My little brother was in charge of exercising Annie."

"Is he a good hand?"

"Sure. He's been riding since before he could walk."

"So he gave Annie a good, hard run?"

"That's what I told him." A suspicious look

came over Tara's face. "Although . . . he is as lazy as a hound dog in the sun."

"Could he have let Annie take it easy?"

Now Tara looked mad. "He could have walked her a mile, and then sat under a tree reading."

"OK," Anya said with a nod. "And did you cut back on Annie's feed?"

"Nope."

"Anything strange about her pee?"

Tara nodded solemnly. "It's been dark red."

Anya let out a heavy sigh. "Tara, Annie has a severe case of Azoturia."

Stella saw all the hope drain out of Tara's face. Josie nodded grimly – as if what Anya had said confirmed her worst fears.

"Do what you can for her," Tara said sadly.

Anya knelt and began pawing through her bag.

Well, the horse people might be following this. But Stella was lost. "What's Azoturia?" she demanded.

"It's a condition that's caused when a horse is fed a working ration, but not exercised sufficiently." Anya pulled some small vials out of her bag. She dropped several into her shirt pocket. She began to draw the contents of one into a syringe.

"Why is that so bad?"

"The horse stores the extra energy in her

muscles," Anya explained. "Then, when you exercise her, too much lactic acid is produced. The lactic acid causes the muscles to release myoglobin. A flood of myoglobin can damage the kidneys."

Whoa, Stella thought. She didn't understand much of what Anya had told her. But she still got the message: Annie was in severe danger.

Anya approached the horse, gave her a quick thump with the back of her hand, and injected her.

"What was that?" Tara asked.

"Painkiller."

Anya slipped the used syringe into a plastic bag and pulled out a clean one. "Tara, fetch a blanket for Annie," she said. "Stella, run to the truck for some IV fluid. Get Josie to help you. I want at least a gallon to start. And bring a gallon of electrolyte solution."

"Where should we meet you?"

"Right here. We can't move her. Not until tomorrow, at least."

Stella and Josie ran.

"I guess Tara won't be able to compete," Stella said as she threw open the back of the truck.

Josie stared at her. "You don't get it, do you?"

"What?"

"Annie might die. If Anya can't get enough of

66

the poison out of her system, her kidneys could shut down."

"Sounds like you've seen it before."

"When I was five. A two-year-old stallion. We called him Fox."

Stella nodded. When Josie was five . . . the same year her mother had died. Losing that horse must have been hard.

"Let's hope Anya can save Annie," Stella said.

"Yup."

They gathered the gear and ran back to the arena. Anya had finished giving Annie her injections. She'd fed a stomach tube through Annie's nose and inserted the IV in her neck.

Meanwhile Jared had run for a ladder.

Anya hung the IV fluid on the ladder above Annie's head. She flushed the electrolyte solution down the tube with a large-dose syringe.

Then Anya stepped back from the horse and watched her. "Looks like the painkillers are working," she commented.

Annie looked a good bit calmer. Her eyes were less wild. And she'd stopped tossing her head. While they were watching, she let loose with a powerful stream of urine. Dark-red urine.

Tara gave Anya a questioning look.

"That's fine," Anya said with a nod. "She's passing the myoglobin. We like that."

"What now?" Tara asked.

Anya shrugged. "We'll keep the IVs going. In about half an hour, we'll give her another infusion through the stomach tube. Mostly we'll wait to see if Annie can stay on her feet for the next twenty-four hours. That's how long it will take for her to expel the toxins."

"Twenty-four hours." Tara rubbed her eyes, but she didn't make any move to leave.

Stella understood how she felt. Twenty-four hours was a long time to wait, wondering if your horse was going to die.

She glanced at her watch. 3:02.

This time tomorrow they'd know if Annie was out of danger.

3:02 . . .

Something about that time sounded familiar. But why? She didn't have to be home all day. And where else could she have to go?

"Oh!" Stella said as it came to her. "Oh, no!"

She scanned the crowd. It had thinned out now that the crisis with Annie had passed. Sure enough, Cora had slipped away.

"What's wrong?" Jared asked.

"Cora's race. We're missing it!"

❧ 8 ❧

Stella, Jared and Josie rushed into the show ring just in time to hear the announcer say, "Ladies and gentlemen, our next rider is a home town gal. Everyone please welcome Miss Cora Sullivan!"

Three fifty-gallon drums had been set out in the ring. The riders had to circle each drum in a cloverleaf pattern. Whoever did it fastest won.

As Cora and Cinnamon burst out of the gate, an electric timer mounted over the stands buzzed loudly and started moving. A readout on the scoreboard showed the time down to a tenth of a second.

"Go, Cora!" Stella hollered.

Josie and Jared yelled too. Everyone was yelling.

Cora headed for the first barrel at a blistering pace.

Josie turned to Stella. "Cinnamon looks nervous."

Stella nodded. The chestnut horse's nostrils

69

were flaring. She had her ears laid back against her head. "Cora can handle her," she said.

Cora and Cinnamon rounded the first barrel – coming close enough to make Stella gasp. Knocking over a barrel would earn Cora a five-second penalty. And that would be enough to make her lose the race.

"What time does she have to beat?" Jared asked.

Josie pointed to the clock. It had a readout that was labelled "BEST TIME: 17:   41."

Cora was heading for the second barrel. She was doing a great job handling Cinnamon, translating all of the horse's nervous energy into speed. The clock read 8:23.

"I think Cora can win this," Josie said.

Stella bit her lip. "If she can control Cinnamon."

"And she doesn't knock over a barrel," Josie added.

"Hey – this is kind of exciting!" Jared said.

"No joke," Josie said.

Cora started back. Stella began bouncing up and down on her tiptoes. This was going to be close.

"Where's Mom and Dad?" Stella asked. "Are they seeing this?"

Dragging her attention away from the course,

70

Stella quickly scanned the crowd. She spotted her parents up in the stands. Papa Pete, Stella's grandfather, was with them. They were on their feet, shouting and cheering. Obviously they realized how close Cora was coming to beating the best time.

Stella turned back to the course. Cora was rounding the last barrel. Cinnamon was tilted at a forty-five degree angle to the ground. As they headed towards home, she straightened up. Cora was leaning forward in the saddle, over the horse's neck. Under her cowboy hat, her hair was blowing back in the wind. Cinnamon's hooves kicked up dirt as she ran. Her legs were blurred by her speed.

14:98.

"Go, Cora!" Stella shouted.

15:17.

"Come on, come on, come on," Jared muttered.

Stella looked back at the clock, back at the course, then back at the clock.

Cinnamon galloped across the finish line.

A buzzer sounded.

The clock stopped.

17:22.

"Yes!" Stella screamed. She and Josie shared an excited hug. Jared was grinning.

"What a fine showing from the home town gal!" the announcer boomed. "Miss Cora Sullivan moves into first place. And now please welcome our next rider . . ."

Stella tuned out the announcer. "Let's go find Cora," she said.

Stella, Jared and Josie caught up with Cora outside the horse barn. She'd dismounted and was walking Cinnamon slowly to cool her down.

"Cora! You were great!" Stella said.

Cora turned to them with an excited smile. She was still breathless from her ride. "Thanks . . ."

"I think you're going to win!" Josie said.

Cora shook her head in happy disbelief. "I

know! Only . . ." Some of the light died out of her eyes. "I wish Tara and Annie Oakley could have raced. Even though they definitely would have beaten us."

Jack, Norma and Papa Pete came rushing up then. Jake from the stables followed. For the next five minutes, everyone relived the race, congratulating Cora and Cinnamon over and over. Eventually, Jake and Cora decided to walk Cinnamon back to the stables.

Things were winding down for the day. The fairway rides and games would stay open well into the night. But the competitions were over until the next morning.

After checking in with Anya – Annie's condition hadn't changed – Stella, Josie and Jared caught a ride home with Stella's parents. Papa Pete took the family out for a fancy steak dinner to celebrate Cora's victory. No one else had beaten her time. At home, Stella walked Rufus and then fell into bed. She drifted off almost immediately and dreamed about a dark-haired woman creeping through town and snatching people's dogs.

On the way to pick up Jared and Josie the next morning, Anya told Stella that she'd moved Annie back to her stall around midnight. Her condition was slowly improving.

Anya had talked to Assistant Sheriff Rose about Rocky that morning. But Sheriff Rose said Mr Naylor hadn't called her.

"That's weird," Stella said. "If someone stole Rufus, I'd call the police right away."

Anya shrugged. "Maybe Mr Naylor isn't feeling well. He probably has a few aches and pains after getting tossed by a buffalo."

Once they got to the fairgrounds, Anya went off to check on Annie. Stella hadn't got a waffle the day before. She bought one, and then wandered with Josie and Jared to the arena.

"What's happening today?" Jared asked eagerly.

"Bull riding," Josie said.

"Cool! Let's get a good seat."

They found seats near the front of the stands. Stella felt a bit uneasy. Bull riding was one of the events Mrs Capra thought was cruel. Stella hoped she wouldn't see any animals mistreated.

Josie and Jared didn't seem worried. They looked around the stands in excitement. The place was packed. About twice as many people had turned up for the second day of competition. And they were still pouring in.

"I don't think I've ever been to a bull-riding competition before," Stella said.

Josie gave her a surprised look. "Really? It's the best part of the rodeo."

Stella shrugged. Her family usually just watched the barrel racing. And then, only if Cora was competing. Jack and Norma weren't bull-riding fans. That thought made Stella even more nervous about what she was about to see.

"Good morning, good people!" the announcer called. "Welcome to the second day of the annual Gateway rodeo!"

The crowd cheered.

"Today's event is a goodie. Bull riding. Now, for you folks who've never been closer to a cow than a milkshake, here's what's goin' to happen. A bunch of crazy fellows are going to take a seat on the back of a bull. And they're going to try to stay up there for eight seconds."

The announcer introduced the first rider. Stella and her friends stood up as the bull charged out of the chute with a cowboy on his back.

A group of musicians sat in the stands on the far side of the arena. Two fiddles and a banjo. They started playing the second the bull burst into the ring.

The bull was a massive freight train of an animal with two-foot-long horns about as big around as Stella's thigh. He came out snorting, head down, and charged into the middle of the arena.

The cowboy was struggling to stay perched on

the bull's bare back. With one gloved hand he was holding on to a rope pulled tightly around the bull's middle. His other hand was high above his head. He sat almost on top of his rope hand, leaning back, balancing.

"He's got to keep his free hand in the air," Josie shouted over the crowd noise. "He gets disqualified if he touches anything with his free hand."

Stella could hardly breathe. Bulls always scared her. And this one looked mean.

"He's a good bull," Josie said appreciatively as the massive animal kicked his back legs and spun in a tight turn.

"Good? He looks deadly," said Jared.

"That's what's good about him," Josie said. "The judges are watching how much the bull bucks. Riders are scored on a scale of one to twenty-five. So are the bulls."

The bull bounced across the ring, tossing the cowboy around like a rag doll. The cowboy's hat fell off. The crowd groaned each time the cowboy hit the bull's back. Stella could imagine how much that had to hurt. The guy was going to have so many bruises he wouldn't be able to sit down.

Suddenly the band stopped.

A buzzer buzzed.

"The eight seconds are up," Josie said. "He can get off now."

"Get off?" Jared repeated.

"Right."

"Isn't that kind of dangerous?" Stella asked.

"Well . . . sometimes," Josie admitted.

The cowboy didn't dismount the way you would smoothly slide off a trained horse. He just let go of the rope and let the bull knock him loose.

He landed on his feet, but stumbled and fell forward.

"Get up," Josie murmured.

The bull snorted. He stared at the cowboy with one dead-looking eye. Then he put his head down and aimed his horns right at the cowboy's stomach.

❦ 9 ❦

The bull charged.

The cowboy scuttled backwards. But he was too slow. The bull hit him in the side, using his horns to flip him over.

"Ohhh . . .," the crowd groaned.

Stella flinched as the bull turned and came back for a second pass. Forget the bulls. Maybe Mrs Capra should worry about the *cowboys* being mistreated.

Jared covered his eyes and whimpered.

Stella wanted to look away, but couldn't. It was like surgery. She was repulsed and fascinated at the same time. The bull was about to stomp on this cowboy. Maybe kill him.

Then something bizarre happened. Someone ran into the centre of the ring, straight for the charging bull. It was . . . a clown! It was Red! He was trying to get the bull's attention.

Stella sprang to her feet. "What is he doing?"

"Cowboy protection," Josie said.

"Cowboy what?"

"Protection. The clown's job is to distract the bull long enough for the cowboy to get up and to safety."

"A clown?" Stella couldn't believe it. But it was working. The bull turned towards Red and started running after him.

Another clown dropped into the arena. He pulled the cowboy to his feet and helped him crawl over the gate.

"He's OK, folks!" the announcer shouted. "Just knocked silly by bull number one oh one."

The crowd started to cheer.

Stella's eyes were glued to the ring. The cowboy was safe, but the bull was still running after Red. Red must have been scared to death. Who wouldn't be? But he didn't show it. He even managed to run funny. He gave the crowd a big wink just before he scrambled over a gate. A second later, the bull crashed into the metal, rattling it.

Jared uncovered his eyes. "This is crazy."

Josie grinned. "That's why people love it."

Stella didn't know if she loved it. She felt about the same way she'd felt after seeing a bad car accident that spring. Horrified. And something else. Something like . . . electrified. That's the thing about fear, she realized. It really wakes you up.

Everyone in the crowd seemed to feel it. They were whooping and hollering as the next bull tore into the ring.

Not all of the rides were as exciting as that first one. Most of the riders fell off before the eight-second buzzer. And most of them got to their feet and out of the ring without any trouble.

The crowd wasn't ugly. They weren't out for blood. But Stella sensed that they knew something bad could happen any second, and that they wanted to be watching if it did. She wasn't any different.

"Hey, look," Josie nudge Stella with her elbow. "A fight."

Stella looked where Josie was pointing. Two angry-looking men were pushing and shoving each other near the chute. Stella could see that they were shouting, but she couldn't hear what they were saying. They were hands – cowboys – with worn hats and boots – not tourists.

"We should do something," Jared said.

"Like what?" Josie asked.

"I'm going to call Anya," Stella said. "She'll know how to get in touch with security." She pulled her walkie-talkie off her belt and explained the situation.

A few moments later, from their perch in the grandstands, Stella and her friends could see Anya striding towards the two men. Assistant Sheriff Rose was with her. By now a crowd was forming around the men.

"Come on," Jared said. "Let's find out what's going on."

"Cool," Josie said.

They were already up and sidestepping their way out of the grandstand. Stella groaned as she got up and followed them. She didn't like fights.

Anya seemed to feel the same way. "Mr Wyatt, this is ridiculous!" she was shouting at the bigger, burlier of the two men as the kids pushed their way through the crowd.

The two men still had their eyes locked on each

other. They looked like they were each waiting for the other to take the first swing.

"Do you know who that is?" Josie whispered excitedly.

"Um, some guy named Mr Wyatt?" Jared guessed.

"*The* Mr Wyatt," Josie said. "He's a stockman. He provided all the rough stock for the rodeo events."

"You call protecting my animals ridiculous?" Mr Wyatt boomed.

"No," Anya said. "But I think we can settle this without violence."

"Tell me what the trouble is," Assistant Sheriff Rose said.

"This here hand hurt my bull!"

"And how'd he do that?" Sheriff Rose's tone was patient.

"Pulled the flank strap too tight!"

"What's a flank strap?" Jared said.

Josie started to answer, but a man in the crowd was faster. "It's a cord tied around the bull's abdomen," he explained.

"Right," Josie agreed.

Jared paled slightly. "Does it go around . . . um, any of the bull's important parts?"

The man chuckled. "Nope."

"What does the strap do?" Stella asked.

Nobody answered. Meanwhile, the hand was raging. "I just pulled it tight enough to make the bull buck. The cowboys want a wild ride. Bucking earns them higher scores."

"My bulls all buck!" Mr Wyatt shouted. "That bull is top quality. He's got heart. He doesn't need to be tortured to perform."

"Listen . . . fine! He's your bull. If you want me to loosen the strap, I'll do it."

"Not good enough," Mr Wyatt said. "That bull is worth thousands, and if he's injured you're going to pay."

Mr Wyatt turned to Assistant Sheriff Rose. "I want to press charges."

"What kind of charges?"

"Vandalism! I don't know. Cruelty to animals. Destruction of property. You pick."

Sheriff Rose smiled ever so slightly "OK. Well, before I do that, why don't we see if the bull has been injured."

"Good idea!" The ranch hand spat out the words.

Sheriff Rose turned to Anya. "Would you do the honours?"

"Sure," Anya said.

Stella's eyes widened as she watched Anya climb the rails of the chute until she was in the same position as the riders just before they climbed on the bull's back.

Anya looked down and pointed at one of the hands. "Could you hold my feet?"

One of the hands – not the one Mr Wyatt was accusing – came forward and grabbed Anya's boots. "If I say pull, get me out of there quick."

"Yes'm." The hand nodded tensely.

The bull turned one eye towards Anya and snorted angrily. He seemed to think Anya was his rider. He grew agitated – pawing the ground with his hooves and banging against the gate with his head.

Stella couldn't take her eyes off the bull's horns. They were long and twisted, the colour of old men's fingernails. Sharp.

The chute was too narrow for the bull to kick Anya. But he could crush her hand simply by moving over against the rail. Stella couldn't even guess what kind of damage he could do with those horns.

❧ **10** ❧

Anya murmured quietly to the bull. She reached way down into the chute to examine the bull's . . . Stella couldn't exactly tell what. Maybe his ribs. Or some internal organ.

The bull grew strangely still. He snorted softly and seemed to be worried about whatever was happening around his belly. His expression seemed to say, What kind of bull rider is *this*?

All it would take was one false move, and Anya would be seriously injured. A slip of the hand's grip. A too-delicate touch that would spook the bull.

But Anya didn't seem worried. At least she wasn't hurrying with the examination. Stella felt like five minutes passed while she breathlessly watched Anya.

"OK, bring me up easy." Anya's voice was muffled.

The hand pulled and Anya's face came back into view.

Stella let out her breath and gave Jared a relieved look.

"Well?" Mr Wyatt demanded.

"He looks good," Anya said as she jumped back to the ground. "No broken ribs. No internal injuries. Although I do think the flank strap is tighter than it needs to be."

Stella saw the red flush drain out of Mr Wyatt's face. As his anger faded, he smiled for the first time. He stepped towards the hand with his own hand extended. "Let's put this behind us," he said. "Truce?"

The two men shook.

"I'll loosen that strap," the hand said.

"Nice work, Anya," Sheriff Rose said.

"That's what I'm here for."

The crowd started to drift back towards the grandstand.

"Come on," Josie said. "I want to see what this bull can do."

"Yeah, let's go," Jared said.

But Anya put a hand on Stella's shoulder. "Got some news for you. Rocky is back at the clinic. I told Travis to call around to the local motels, and see if he can locate Mr Naylor."

Stella felt a surge of relief. "That's great!"

Anya nodded. "The woman who picked him up brought him back. He tore out some of his stitches."

"We have to go back to the clinic," Stella said. She nodded at Sheriff Rose. "*All* of us."

"This is the stolen bulldog?" Sheriff Rose asked.

Anya nodded.

"OK then," Sheriff Rose said. "I'll meet you back at the clinic."

Josie and Jared stayed at the rodeo. Anya and Stella climbed into the 4 x 4 for the trip to the clinic.

A dark-haired woman with oversized sunglasses was sitting in the waiting room. Stella thought she would run when she saw them. But she smiled pleasantly. "Are you the vet?" she asked.

"Yes."

Travis came out of the office. "Rocky is in the examination room."

"I'd better look at him right away." Anya moved quickly down the hallway. Normally, Stella would have followed. But now she hesitated. She didn't want to leave the dark-haired woman alone. What if she disappeared before Sheriff Rose got here?

The woman's smile was beginning to look strained. "May I . . . help you somehow?" she asked Stella.

Stella realized she was staring. She couldn't

help it. She kept wondering what kind of person stole someone else's dog. This woman didn't even seem to feel bad about it. At least, she didn't look guilty.

"You're Rocky's owner?" she asked.

"Well, yes. In a manner of speaking."

"What does *that* mean?" Stella asked.

"I'm sorry." The woman's tone was frosty. "Have we met?" Clearly, she didn't like answering questions from a kid.

"No," Stella said. "I don't know who you are. But I know *what* you are."

The woman looked surprised. And annoyed.

"And what is that?"

"A dognapper!"

"Stella," Travis said. "Maybe we should wait for Anya."

But Stella heard footsteps on the porch. That had to be Assistant Sheriff Rose coming to arrest the dognapper.

"Young lady, I assure you I did not steal Rocky."

"Yeah, right."

"If Rocky isn't my dog, then whose dog is he?"

"Mr Naylor's."

"Mr – who is Mr Naylor?"

The door opened. Everyone turned to look. Stella was surprised when Mr Naylor – not Sheriff Rose – walked into the waiting room.

"Mr Naylor," Stella said. "This is the woman who stole your dog."

The woman burst into laughter. "Naylor? Where did you get that name, Bob?"

Mr Naylor gave Stella a puzzled look. "Did you tell this woman my name was Bob?"

"No."

The dark-haired woman shook her head and laughed. "Bob, really. Give it up. The gig is done."

Mr Naylor turned to Stella. "Gig?" He shrugged broadly, as if to say the woman was nuts.

Stella didn't know what to make of this. She looked at Travis for help. But he looked just as puzzled as she felt.

"One of you has to be lying," Stella insisted. "Now who owns Rocky?"

"I do," the dark-haired woman said.

"I do," Mr Naylor said.

Stella groaned. She was getting very frustrated. Which is why she felt like hugging Assistant Sheriff Rose when she came through the door.

Sheriff Rose was all business. "Mr Naylor, I work for the local sheriff's office," she said formally. "Stella tells me this woman stole your bulldog. Would you like to press charges?"

Mr Naylor cocked his beefy head to one side. He considered for a moment, a strange smile playing on his lips. "Yes. Yes, I believe I would."

The dark-haired woman stamped her foot. "Bob, really, you're going too far." She turned to Assistant Sheriff Rose. "That dog belongs to me. Or, rather, to my employer. My name is Maggie Grillo and I work for the Denver Bulldogs. Rocky is our mascot."

"That's not true," Stella said. "Mr Naylor is the one who works for the Bulldogs. He told me."

The dark-haired woman gave Stella an exasperated look. "'Mr Naylor' may have told you that, but 'Mr Naylor' is a liar. If you look in

90

his wallet, you'll see that all of his IDs say Bob Burford."

"That doesn't prove—" the fat man started.

The dark-haired woman began searching through her purse. "I have my ID badge in here. If you don't believe me about the dog, call my boss. He'll *fax* you Rocky's registration."

Stella felt a prick of doubt. The dark-haired woman sounded awfully convincing. And Mr Naylor wasn't doing much – except standing there looking like he was trying to come up with a plausible lie.

"I'd like to see both your wallets."

"But—" Mr Naylor started.

"Don't argue with me!" Sheriff Rose said sharply.

Mr Naylor took a step back and held up both hands. "OK, OK. I'm beat. Rocky belongs to Maggie. Or her boss. Or the Bulldogs' six fans."

"Hey!" Maggie said. "That's not fair. We have eight fans ever since we hired a publicist."

Mr Naylor, Bob – whoever he was – wagged one finger in Maggie's face. "Don't think this means that the Bulldogs are going to beat us in the play-offs."

"I don't have to think it. I know it!"

Mr Naylor – or whatever his name was – started to move towards the door.

Assistant Sheriff Rose reached out one hand and grabbed his meaty upper arm. "Not so fast." She looked at Maggie. "You pressing charges?"

Maggie and Bob both got a good laugh out of that.

"No," Maggie said. "Bob would just return the favour next time I borrow Pete."

"Who's Pete?" Stella was almost afraid to ask.

"A prairie dog," Maggie said wearily.

"Not just any prairie dog!" the fat man boomed. "The fairest prairie dog in the universe. And the beautiful mascot of the Colorado Springs Dogs, the best farm league team to ever grace a western state."

"You can go now, Bob," Maggie said.

"Please," Sheriff Rose put in.

And he did.

Rocky survived.

Anya stitched him up without any problem. She wanted to keep him overnight, but Maggie said that was impossible. Apparently there were six other teams in their baseball league. That meant there were six other "Bobs" lurking around, trying to steal other teams' mascots and ruin their players' morale.

In the end, Anya gave Maggie a long list of instructions and sent Rocky home with her.

Anya and Stella made it back to the rodeo just as the closing day parade was ending. Stella found Jared and Josie on the fairway – whooping and hollering as the cowboys, riders and clowns passed. They looked worn out but happy.

"How'd you like the rodeo?" Stella asked Jared.

"I can't wait until next summer!"

Stella smiled. Jared had caught rodeo fever.

"There's your sister!" Josie shouted.

Stella looked up and saw Cora riding by on
Cinnamon. They were proudly wearing their first-
place ribbons. Cinnamon seemed to realize that
she was on display. She was prancing and tossing
her head. For a horse, she was a real flirt.

The parade was great. But then the group got a
real disappointment: the fireworks were cancelled
because of fire hazard. The weather was so hot
and dry that Gateway's fire chief was afraid a
stray spark would set the woods near the
fairgrounds aflame.

The good news was that Annie Oakley was
going to survive. She'd never recover completely,
but Anya said Tara was happy to be taking her

horse home. On the other hand, she'd expressed a desire to leave her lazy little brother in Gateway.

Stella got home earlier than she expected – just in time to see Norma pulling out of the driveway in her Park Service truck. Norma braked, and Stella steered her bike up next to the driver's window.

"Where are you going?" Stella asked.

"To drop dinner off to a friend – Juliet."

"Cool."

"Want to come?"

"You bet."

Stella ran into the house and put on her hiking boots, clean shorts and a fresh T-shirt. Then she ran back outside and climbed into the truck. After spending two days in the fairgrounds, getting out to the woods would be nice. And they had plenty of time for a quick hike. The sun wouldn't set until almost nine.

Norma turned on to the road. Both windows in the truck were down. Wind rushed in, but Stella still felt hot and dusty. She found herself thinking about big, tall glasses of ice water. Rushing rivers. Popsicles.

The very air seemed to be radiating heat. Stella's hair felt like straw after baking in the sunshine all day.

Huge, dark cumulus clouds were forming on

the horizon. They were light-coloured close to the ground, but the tops were flattened out and ominous-looking. As Norma pulled off the road to the trailhead, lightning flashed.

"Hey!" Stella popped off her seat belt. "I think it's going to rain."

"Wouldn't that be nice." Norma sighed. "Hasn't rained since May. But I think we're just in for some dry lightning."

Norma had a water cooler in the back of the truck. They each drank half a litre of water before starting out. Then Norma picked up her pack, which contained a huge chunk of fresh elk meat.

"Oof," Norma groaned. "This is heavy."

"Why don't I take the water?" Stella offered.

"Thanks." Norma pulled three litre bottles out of her pack and transferred them into Stella's.

They set out.

The trail up to the pen was faint, but it was beginning to be familiar to Stella. She let Norma lead the way, easily falling into step beside her.

"Mom, do you think rodeos are cruel?" she asked.

Norma didn't answer right away. "Well, I wouldn't say so. The animals are usually well treated. I mean, they have to be. Some of those rodeo bulls are worth more than our house."

Stella walked in silence for a few minutes. The

light had a strange yellowish colour as it came through the dark clouds, and it cast long shadows.

"How come you never took me to a bull-riding competition?" Stella asked.

"Well . . . I don't enjoy it. It's a bit brutal for my taste. I prefer events where people work with animals, not against them. Events like barrel racing are more my speed."

"Marisa and Mrs Capra were boycotting the rodeo."

"I'm not surprised. But I'd be sad if rodeo totally disappeared. It's part of our western culture. Something that's one hundred per cent American. Like baseball."

"More like the Indy Five Hundred."

"Or boxing. Or ice hockey when the gloves come off."

"I'm not sure I like any of those things," Stella said. "Well, except baseball."

"You don't have to."

Stella was lost in thought, trying to figure out why people liked danger. Why they liked the idea of seeing someone else get hurt.

And then . . .

Flash! Rrrr! CRRRACCK! BOOOOM!

❧ 12 ❧

The sound was deafening. Stella jumped about a foot, shaking. She saw Norma stumble.

Stella rushed forward and grabbed her mum around the waist. The sound came from everywhere at once. A few seconds passed before it slowly faded out. The air was full of energy. It smelled charged – like a clothes dryer left running too long.

"What was that?" Stella demanded. But she knew. It was lightning, and it had hit somewhere close. Stella's ears were ringing.

Norma smoothed Stella's hair. "You OK?"

Stella nodded.

"I think lighting hit that pine." Norma pointed and started walking towards a tree about fifteen metres off to the side of the trail.

Stella followed, expecting to see a burned out tree like the dozens she'd seen in the woods over the years. But this pine wasn't burned out. It was *burning*. Well, more like *smouldering*.

The trunk looked as if a bomb had exploded inside. A huge crack had opened, exposing pale inner wood. When they got closer, Stella could see that several large limbs had broken off. Burning bark had scattered in all directions.

"Should we put the fire out?" Stella asked.

"No," Norma said. "We don't have any tools. And besides, it's a natural fire. Park Service policy is to let naturally occurring fires burn."

Stella couldn't take her eyes off the fire. The pine needles were smoking. Some burst into flames while Stella was watching.

"Mom?" Stella said. She was trying to keep the fear out of her voice. But that one word came out kind of shaky.

"Hey, Muffin – don't worry," Norma said. "We're going to be fine. I'm a trained firefighter, remember?" Norma held up her arms like a weight lifter.

Stella forced a smile. She knew her mum had been a smokejumper while she was in graduate school. Smokejumpers are firefighters who parachute into burning forests.

Stella nodded, trying to calm down. But it was hard to relax. The fire was spreading fast, creeping through the dry brown pine needles.

"The safest place to be in a forest fire is at the fire's tail," Norma said. "Fires usually burn uphill, so we'll stand downhill from the lightning-struck pine."

"Can't we just leave?" Stella asked.

"Not yet," Norma said. "I'm going to call fire dispatch and report this. You can keep an eye on the fire. Let me know if the wind starts pushing it any way but uphill."

"You mean the fire might start burning towards us?"

"It could. Especially with these erratic winds."

"What then?"

"Then we'll scramble around and get behind it again."

"OK," Stella whispered. She licked her lips and focused on the fire. Smoke was beginning to swirl through the trees – almost like grey fog. Moving slowly like a ghost hovering just above the ground.

Norma dialled a number on her mobile. She listened, pushed a button, listened some more. "Reggie? Hey – this is Norma Sullivan. From Goldenrock." Pause. "Fine, thanks. Listen, I want to report a lightning-struck pine about a mile northeast of the access road south of Route 2A."

Stella waited patiently while her mother listened. She could smell the fire now. The odour was like smoky pine. Like cigar smoke. A pleasant smell – except for the fact that Stella's brain kept screaming "danger!" The smoke was stinging her eyes, making them water.

"Conditions are severely dry." Norma said into the phone. "The fire is spreading rapidly in heavy fuel. Winds are calm at the moment, although they could gust up. We have an evil-looking thunder cloud overhead."

It was strange. Stella had waited impatiently hundreds of times while Norma, Jack or Anya talked on the phone. She felt the same way she always did. Twitchy. Aggravated. Only this time the reason was slightly more serious. She wanted her mum to get off the phone and get her out of there.

Although . . . the fire *was* fascinating to watch.

Each time the wind gusted, the flames claimed a little more ground. Stella noticed that the fire was starting to take on a rough V shape. The lightning-struck pine was at the point and the flames widened out as they raced up the hill. Stella was glad the fire was going where her mum said it would.

The lower limbs of the lightning-struck pine were burning steadily now. Then, with a soft rushing sound – waaaooof! – the top of the tree went up in flames.

Stella jumped back, staring. The pine looked like an enormous torch.

"You OK, Muffin?" Norma called.

"I – um, yes." Stella had to raise her voice so that her mum could hear her over the crinkling flames.

"That was a good one." Norma gave her a reassuring smile and turned back to her phone conversation. "I suggest putting out a hiker advisory immediately. And I think we should request a monitoring team."

WAAAOOOF! The crown of another tree, slightly higher on the slow burst into flames.

Stella was suddenly aware of being hot. Of course, after a week of ninety-degree heat she was used to being hot. But she was sweating more than usual. Sweat was dripping down her legs and soaking her socks.

Norma was watching the fire now too. She took a couple of steps closer to Stella while continuing her conversation. "No, the Park Service doesn't have any major structures in this area, although we have some very valuable animals penned nearby."

Stella spun around, alarmed. She had forgotten about Juliet and the pups. What would happen if the fire spread all the way to their pen? They had to do something!

Norma made a wry face at Stella. "Gee, Reggie, that's supposed to be a secret."

Stella didn't care if fire dispatch knew about Juliet. Not if they could do something to help her.

"Off the record, yes," Norma said. "Wolf seven and her pups. We've kept the brush cleared around their pen, but I'd feel a whole lot better if we could get some smokejumpers in here to cut a fire line around it."

Stella nodded vigorously. She knew what a fire line was – a strip of ground that had been cleared of all vegetation. Fire can't cross the line because there's no fuel to burn.

"Can the jumpers get in here in time?" Norma said. "We've only got about another seventy-five minutes of sunlight. Sure. OK."

Norma turned off the phone. "He's going to call the smokejumper base," she explained.

"Can we go now?"

"Not yet. Fire dispatch wants us to stick around and monitor the fire."

"Mom, aren't you scared?"

"Nah. I've been in worse than this."

"Like what?"

"Sagebrush fire. Colorado. That stuff burns wicked hot."

"So we're not going to die?"

Norma laughed. "No. But it looks like we're going to be late for dinner."

Stella let out a breath. She felt as if she'd been holding it for twenty minutes. Her shoulders – which had been hunched up to her ears – relaxed back into their normal position.

"How long will we have to wait?"

"If the smokejumpers come, they should be here within an hour. After that it will be too dark for them to parachute in. If dispatch sends a ground crew, we could be waiting a couple of hours."

Stella nodded. Even though she was scared, she was willing to stay in the woods all night if it would help Juliet. "What if the fire reaches the pen before then?" she asked.

"Shouldn't," Norma said. But Stella thought

she heard a note of worry in her voice.

Norma sat down on a flat rock and got the water out of Stella's pack. She offered Stella some and drank a little herself. Then she rummaged around in her pack until she came up with a couple of bandannas. She doused them with water.

"Put this around your mouth and nose," Norma said. "I don't want you inhaling too much smoke."

Stella wrapped the bandanna around her face. Now the smell of the smoke was mixed with the smell of fabric softener. Norma tied on her own bandanna. She looked like a bandit.

Norma and Stella didn't talk much after that. They sat facing the fire, watching the flames flicker. The torched-up pines burned brightly for fifteen minutes, the flames shooting way up into the sky. Then, slowly, the flames began to die down.

Stella crept forward and examined the burned-out area. The ground beneath the pines was scorched and hot. But the trees were still standing. They still looked strong. Stella was wondering if they would grow back.

After half an hour, Norma called fire dispatch and told them the fire was spreading quickly and now covered about three acres. By the time she got off the phone, the light was fading out of the sky.

"Reggie says the smokejumpers are on their way," Norma reported. "But he's still not sure if they have enough light to jump. It is going to be a race against the sun."

Stella couldn't see the sun, but she could see that the woods were growing darker. The flames seemed to dance, giving off a mesmerizing light.

Then Stella noticed something strange. The forest was oddly quiet.

Usually, at dusk, you'd hear birds mostly. Swarms of swallows would be making a racket as they scooped insects out of the air. The evening's mosquitoes and moths would also attract thousands of bats. You could hear their wings beating if you got close.

Or you'd catch the faint scuffling of squirrels, voles, chipmunks, marmots and mice as they gathered food. Deer would be feeding and you might hear one pushing through the under-growth.

Now there was no sound except for the crackling flames.

No bark beetles clicking.

No frogs singing.

Nothing but crinkle, crinkle, crinkle.

"Mom, what's going to happen to the

animals?" Stella asked.

"Oh, they should be fine," Norma said. "Wild animals know how to protect themselves from fire. Birds fly away. Voles, mole, and rabbits stay underground while the fire burns over them. Frog and fish are fine underwater."

Stella accepted that, but she knew she wouldn't be able to relax until the fire was out for good.

Another half an hour passed.

"Hey, Stella – look!" Norma scrambled to her feet.

Stella looked up through the trees. "I don't see anything." She stood up and peered into the darkening sky.

Norma came right up behind her and pointed. "There."

Now Stella thought she saw it. Something was hurtling towards the earth. Something like a big yellow rock – a rock with a helmet.

"Is – is that a smokejumper?" Stella asked.

"Yup!"

The jumper's rectangular parachute suddenly opened, pulling him higher into the air. Now he floated down lazily.

"He's lost," Stella said. "He's heading towards the top of the mountain."

"To the pen."

"Oh," Stella said. "Right." Somehow she had

imagined that the smokejumpers were going to land right next to them. Now she could see another one falling. And another. She stopped to count. There were six jumpers altogether.

Norma and Stella watched until they disappeared into the woods. "Are we hiking up to meet them?" Stella asked.

"No," Norma said. "I don't want you anywhere near the head of this fire. And besides, it's time you were in bed."

"What about Juliet's dinner?" Stella asked.

"That can wait until the fire has burned around the pen. It'll be safe to go up there tomorrow or the next day. Let's go home."

"OK." Stella agreed.

But they stood staring at the flames for a few more minutes before heading downhill.

Rodeos

Characters in this book have several different opinions about rodeos.

Josie loves them.

Marisa thinks they're cruel.

Stella wants to learn more about them before making a decision. But even after spending a weekend attending a rodeo and considering what she sees, she isn't entirely sure what to think.

What's your opinion? To help you decide, here is some information about the history of the rodeo and how rodeo animals are treated today.

Contests of Skill

More than a hundred and thirty years ago, cowboys set out on long and lonely cattle drives across hundreds of miles of open prairie. The cowboys rode for weeks – sleeping outside, getting dusty and dirty, and eating food cooked over open fires. They had only a few other men for company and very little entertainment.

When the cowboys finally reached the end of the trail after all that hard riding, they were ready to celebrate. Their celebrations often included contests of skill. These contests allowed them to show off how well they could handle livestock. Eventually these contests grew into rodeos.

The First Rodeo?

Many towns in the western United States claim to be the first to hold a rodeo. Among them are Cheyenne, Wyoming and Winfield, Kansas. A rodeo held in Denver, Colorado in 1887 was the first with paying spectators.

That handful of paying spectators started a huge trend. In a recent year, twenty-two *million* fans plunked down money to attend rodeos. Each year 46 states and four Canadian provinces hold rodeos. In addition, approximately 500 schools and clubs hold junior rodeos for younger participants.

Spurs, Straps and Rules

So do these popular events cause harm to animals? That depends on who you ask. People who oppose rodeos generally point to three events that seem particularly hard on animals: calf-roping, steer-wrestling and bull riding. Here's a description of these events and an explanation of how rodeo organizers attempt to protect the animals:

Calf-roping
What happens? A calf is released from a chute and chased by a cowboy on horseback. The cowboy must lasso the animal around the neck. Once the lasso is in place, the horse skids to a stop – forcing the calf to stop running. The rider leaps from the horse's saddle and throws the calf to the ground. To get points, the cowboy must tie any three of the calf's legs together within 30 seconds of the calf being released from the chute.
What seems cruel? The sudden jerk that stops the running calf.
What protects the animals? Rodeo rules require that a roping device be attached to the rider's saddle. This device makes it impossible to pull too hard on the calf's neck. Cowboys are disqualified if the calf is yanked off its feet. In general, lassoes are a common part of ranch life and don't seem to harm the rough animals.

Steer-wrestling
What happens? A steer is released and chased by two riders. One rider keeps the steer running in a

straight line while the other grabs the steer by the horns and leaps from his or her horse. The second rider twists the steer's neck to force him to fall to the ground. The contestant has 30 seconds from the time the steer is released to wrestle him to the ground.

What seems cruel? This event may cause strained muscles and tendons in the steers' necks. (Not to mention the cowboys'!)

What protects the animals? Their own strength. Steers weigh up to around 450 kilograms. It isn't easy to prove that a cowboy could harm such a big, aggressive animal with his bare hands.

Bull riding

What happens? Cowboys ride a bull bareback for eight seconds. They win up to 25 points by staying on the bull's back. The cowboy earns up to an additional 25 points if the bull he or she is riding bucks and twists violently.

What seems cruel? Bull riders spur their mounts – that is, they run metal star-shaped wheels (worn on the heels of their boots) over the backs of the bulls to encourage them to buck. Also, "flank straps" are tied around the bulls' abdomens. The straps anger the bulls. Again, the purpose is to encourage bucks and twists in the ride.

What protects the animals? Rodeo rules say spurs

must be blunt and loose so that they roll. Flank straps cannot contain sharp or cutting objects. Also, bulls come equipped with a thick skin. Bull hide is about seven times as thick as human skin. Rodeo officials say that spurs and straps that would hurt humans are no big deal for bulls.

Do the Rules Work?

Statistics show that very few animals suffer serious injuries at rodeos. One recent survey examined about 34,000 animals that participated in 28 professional rodeos. Less than one animal in 2,000 was injured.

However, it does seem fair to say that the animals are irritated, bruised and scared in some events. Other events – like barrel racing, for example – draw little complaint. Animals must be in top physical shape to perform well in timed races like these.

It's difficult to imagine that rodeo professionals would intentionally put their animals – especially bulls and horses – at risk. Some bulls are almost as famous as the cowboys and cowgirls who ride them. Each year, the Professional Rodeo Cowboys Association elects a bull of the year. Bodacious, a bull that won two years in a row, was popular enough to have his own fan club and to appear in *Sports Illustrated*. He earned big bucks by serving as a "spokesbull" for Dodge trucks and other products. These days he is enjoying a comfortable retirement on a ranch in Texas.

Calves, which are eventually slaughtered for meat, may not be treated as well. And animals in smaller, less well-regulated rodeos may have a rougher time than the animals in big national events. Some people might argue that rodeo rules should be stricter and put a greater emphasis on helping the animals *before* they get hurt, not on punishing cowboys after it's too late to stop the animals' suffering.

EMILY COSTELLO

Animal Emergency 4
Runaway Wolf

Romeo, one of the wild wolves in Goldenrock Park, has been shot – and Stella is determined to help catch the culprit. Some people just don't want the wolves around – and they'd do anything to get rid of them.

When Romeo's mate goes missing with her litter of tiny pups. Stella knows she's got to find her – before the hunter strikes again . . .

EMILY COSTELLO

Animal Emergency 6
Kitten Crisis

A fire is raging through the forest, and Anya's
surgery is full of animals injured by the blaze.
But there's always room for one more, and
Sooty, a lost kitten, urgently needs Stella's
help.

When the fire changes direction, and heads
towards the surgery, it's not just Sooty that's
in danger. It's up to Anya and Stella to save all
the patients – before the whole place goes up
in smoke.

ANIMAL EMERGENCY
titles available from Macmillan

1. Abandoned Puppy	0 330 39354 5	£2.99
2. Otter Alert	0 330 39355 3	£2.99
3. Bad Luck Lion	0 330 39356 1	£2.99
4. Runaway Wolf	0 330 39357 X	£2.99
5. Rabbit Rescue	0 330 39358 8	£2.99
6. Kitten Crisis	0 330 39359 6	£2.99

All Macmillan titles can be ordered at your local bookshop
or are available by post from:

Book Service by Post
PO Box 29, Douglas, Isle of Man IM99 1BQ

Credit cards accepted. For details:
Telephone: 01624 675137
Fax: 01624 670923
E-mail: bookshop@enterprise.net

Free postage and packing in the UK.
Overseas customers: add £1 per book (paperback)
and £3 per book (hardback).

The prices shown are correct at the time of going to press. However,
Macmillan Publishers reserve the right to show new retail prices on
covers which may differ from those previously advertised.